If You Disobey...

*

The Whoopee Cushion

*

Tinker, the Reindeer Who Made a Mess of Things

*

Collection of short stories for children

By

Lili Rhoss

DEDICATION

To my grandchildren –

Brianna, Catrin, Cerian, Bethan, Rhys, Sian.

CONTENTS

1. If You Disobey...

Not far from Brocky Bridge is a peaceful place called Bluebell Dell. It was here that Mother Badger built her sett in the soft brown earth and who, a month or so ago, gave birth to her cubs, Haze and Fog. As usual they slept the day away and sounds of squeaks, snuffles and snores drifted out from the sett. Later as dusk fell, Mother Badger led her cubs out of the sett into the cool, fresh, night air. After a good shake and a scratch they all began to forage for food in the fields and wood nearby. Haze stayed close to his mother, Fog didn't. Instead he charged ahead of her even though he knew his mother wanted her cubs to stay by her side at all times but, as usual, he thought otherwise.

***

Fog waggled his snout about and smelled the earthy woodland smells he loved so much. He scuffed through the fallen twigs and scattered them. He pounced on the bluebells and flattened them. He darted about a bog as he chased a frog. He hunted for moles and chased rabbits down their holes. He saw a hedgehog, prickles and all, but when he sniffed it, it turned into a ball.

As the cubs slurped wiggly worms and slippery slugs up their snouts, they noticed the beams of white light which now and again swished across the hedgerows near Brocky Bridge. Mother Badger saw them too and growled a low growl, a growl which meant 'Danger, do NOT go near.' Haze accepted this without question. Fog didn't. He wondered why the beams of white light were dangerous and decided he would disobey his mother and find out later.

***

In the early hours of the morning, with bellies full after a successful forage, the badgers returned to their sett, replaced their bedding with fresh grass and leaves, then snuggled down together. When Fog thought his mother and brother were asleep, he crept from the sett into the dark night and ran along the woodland path towards Brocky Bridge. Haze opened one eye, watched Fog leave, and even though he knew he was disobeying his mother too, decided

3

to follow to see where his brother was going, and why. Despite feeling guilty at leaving his mother's side Haze followed Fog at a distance and kept out of sight in the shadows. Haze watched Fog as he clawed his way up the muddy bank on to Brocky Bridge. He saw Fog raise his head and look up towards the hedgerows. It was then that Haze realised Flog was looking for the beams of white light to swish across them, but it was Haze who saw them, not Fog, as he had begun to cross the road.

***

Fog was in the middle of the road when he heard the faint noise of a machine and saw two small white eyes coming towards him. He stopped and stared at them. The white eyes stared back at him and got bigger, brighter and closer. Dazzled by the bright eyes, Fog felt the ground shake beneath his paws as the machine noise got louder and louder. Then BANG! Fog was hit high up into the air and landed with a thud in a clump of bluebells at the side of the road. Haze gasped in horror and trembled with fear as he watched the machine roar on by with a windy

whoosh, then he watched its two little red eyes until they disappeared around the bend. He heard Fog whimper and saw him slowly close his eyes. Haze crept out of the shadows and sniffed Fog's warm body. Fog lay still, and silent. Haze nudged his brother but Fog did not respond. Fear gripped Haze as he turned away from his silent brother, slipped down the muddy bank, and ran as fast as he could back to the sett in Bluebell Dell to fetch Mother Badger.

***

At the time Haze ran back to Bluebell Dell to fetch his mother Mr Harry the vet got into his car at Gorse Farm, not far from Brocky Bridge. He'd had an emergency callout and just delivered a new born calf. Now, satisfied that all was well, he was anxious to get back to his home in the village. When he switched on his car's headlights two beams of white light lit up the cowshed, and as the car turned out of the farmyard the beams of white light swished across the hedgerows. At Brocky Bridge the car's white headlights shone on the lifeless cub lying at the side of the road. Mr Harry stopped his car and got out. As he bent down to examine the cub he wondered why he was out on his own, as mother badgers were very protective of their young. It was obvious to Mr Harry that the cub was concussed, possibly hit by a vehicle very recently. He thought the cub might even have internal injuries so an examination and x-ray in his village surgery was inevitable. Gently Mr Harry lifted the little cub's warm, limp body, wrapped him in an old piece of blanket then laid him carefully on the car seat. When Mr Harry drove along the winding road towards his home in the village, two beams of white light from his headlights once again swished across the hedgerows.

***

As Mr Harry drove back to his village surgery with Fog, Haze and his mother scrambled up the muddy bank on to Brocky Bridge. Haze smelled a strange scent as he crept to the spot where he had last seen Fog, but, to his surprise, his brother had gone and all that was there was a flattened patch of bluebells. Mother Badger smelled her little cub's scent on the flattened bluebells and also smelled the strong scent of man who could, and sometimes would, harm badgers. She growled a low growl of danger as she wondered what man had done with her cub. Feeling afraid, she nudged Haze back to the safety of their sett. There they snuggled close together and thought of Fog and where he could be.

***

In his surgery in the village, and watched closely by his cat Puffin, Mr Harry examined Fog. The x-rays showed no broken bones and Mr Harry found no internal injuries. He thought the cub had had a lucky escape as he could easily have been killed. But for now Mr Harry decided to let nature take its course and was sure the cub would recover by morning. He put the unconscious cub into a wire cage to keep him safe, covered him with the old piece of blanket, then secured the catch in the lid. He knew the mother would be looking for her cub so would return him to Brocky Bridge in the early morning. Mr Harry climbed the stairs, switched on his bedroom light and got ready for bed. Downstairs, click-click went the cat flap as Puffin stepped through it into the cool night air.

***

Back in the sett Haze snuggled close to his

mother. He couldn't understand where Fog had gone and thought perhaps it was something to do with the strange scent at Brocky Bridge. Where had he smelled that scent before? Then he remembered. It had been in the village at the end of the wood. *Could Fog be there?* he wondered. Haze decided he was going to find out. He didn't really want to disobey his mother again but he knew in his heart that he had to find Fog. So before dawn, as Mother Badger slept fitfully, he crept out of the sett and ran along the woodland path towards the village. The trees rustled and creaked, the owls hooted, the bats squeaked but, alone and frightened though he was, Haze kept on running.

***

Fog had woken earlier with a sore head and felt quite woozy. His snout wrinkled in disgust at the smell on the old blanket around him and the strong scent of cat. There were other smells too, ones that he had never smelled before. And why were there wire walls all around him? The last thing he remembered doing was crossing the road when he saw two white eyes which got bigger, brighter and closer, which dazzled him, and then the ground began to tremble as a machine noise got louder. Did the big white eyes make the beams of white light which swished across the hedgerows? If so, Mother Badger was right they were they were very dangerous indeed. Fog felt alone as he laid his head on his paws and felt warm tears trickle down his cheeks.

***

When Haze reached the village, strange scents like the one at Brocky Bridge wafted up his snout. Among them was a trace of Fog's familiar scent. It was coming from the house across the road, the one with a light in the upstairs window. Haze waited, watched and listened by the side of the road. He saw beams of white light swish across the hedgerows, then two small white eyes came into view. He heard the roar of a machine and crouched down low. The roar got louder and the two white eyes got bigger, brighter and closer. Then, with a windy whoosh, the machine passed by and Haze watched its two little red eyes disappear round the bend. When no other beams of white light swished across the hedgerows he darted across the road, and into the garden. He sniffed the air and again smelled Fog's familiar scent, which was a little stronger now. Waggling his snout about, he followed the scent across the garden to the back door and looked at a small square flap in front of him. Then he wrinkled his nose in disgust at the strong scent of cat coming from it. But he was certain Fog was somewhere behind the small square flap. Gently Haze nudged it with his snout. It clicked open a little bit and, as well as Fog's scent, the strange scent like the one at Brocky Bridge shot up his snout. Click went the square flap as he pushed it further and saw Fog lying down with wire walls all around him.

***

Fog heard the click-click of the small square flap in the back door and froze with fright at the strange sound. Then he smelled a familiar scent coming through it. It belonged to Haze! Fog squealed with delight at the sight of Haze's snout and, despite feeling woozy, bounced about the cage with joy.

Haze tumbled through the small square flap and skidded across the slippery surgery floor. Quickly he encircled the wire walls as he frantically tried to find a way to release Fog. Then Haze saw the catch and pushed it with his snout. It didn't open. He clouted it hard with his paw. It still didn't open. Then he gripped it with his teeth and waggled his head furiously from side to side. Suddenly the catch snapped open, the lid popped up and out staggered Fog. Quickly the two cubs skidded and scampered across slippery floor, squeezed one after the other through the cat flap, and tumbled out into the cool night air.

***

As the pink of dawn coloured the sky the two cubs ran across Mr Harry's garden, and Haze growled a low growl of danger when they reached the side of the road. Fog now knew he had to heed this growl and so stayed beside his brother. Together they looked for beams of white light to swish across the hedgerows, but when none appeared, Hazy, closely followed by Fog, darted across the road and on to the woodland path towards Bluebell Dell. Fox waggled his snout about, savouring once again the earthy, musty woodland smells he knew so well. Then he smelled the scent he loved most of all, the scent of Mother Badger. And, just as Mr Harry had thought, she was walking up the middle of the woodland path looking for her cubs, waiting for them to come home.

THE END

2. The Whoopee Cushion

"BUT I WANT to go and play in the park with my friends!" argued Jack, as he stamped his feet in anger which made his socks sag.

"Well you can't," said his mother. "Father O'Toole and my sister Agatha are coming to tea and I want you to be there and that's final. Now go upstairs and put a clean T-shirt on, that one is filthy."

***

Jack stomped up the stairs to his bedroom. Kojo, Jack's faithful, hairy mongrel, raced after him and sat beside the bed.

"It's not fair!" said Jack, as he ripped off his grubby T-shirt and kicked it into the corner. "Dad's always at work when Father O'Toole comes, he's lucky." Jack grabbed a clean T-shirt out of a drawer. "But I'm glad Aunt Agatha's coming, she's a good sport and she also thinks priests talk a lot of hot air."

Kojo tilted his head to one side and watched Jack shove his arms angrily through the sleeves of his clean T-shirt. "Well if Mother is making me stay in I'll do something to make her wish I'd gone out. I've got a plan which will really embarrass her. Come on boy, let's put it into action!"

Kojo's heart sank. Jack's doings often resulted in him taking the blame. What was Jack going to do anyway, how was he going to embarrass his mother?

***

Kojo soon found out. He watched as Jack opened the bedside cupboard, rifled among the contents, threw some of them on the floor, then pulled out a round, rubber whoopee cushion. *Oh no, not THAT!* thought Kojo. He watched as Jack took a deep breath then blew air into the whoopee cushion's spout. As jack blew, the whoopee cushion grew bigger and bigger, bigger than Kojo had ever seen it.

***

Then Jack gently squeezed a little air out of the whoopee cushion. It made a very rude noise. Jack giggled. Kojo's heart sank. "When I was a toddler and made rude body noises in my nappy, which sounded just like that, my dad used to call them little gustoes!" said Jack. Clutching the whoopee cushion ever so gently so that no more air escaped, Jack and

Kojo crept down the stairs. After Jack had made sure his mother was still in the kitchen and out of sight, he carefully slid the whoopee cushion underneath the flowery one on Father O'Toole's favourite armchair in the sitting room, the one he always sat on when he came to tea.

***

With a sigh and a feeling of impending doom Kojo flopped down on the rug in front of the sitting room fire.

Pleased with himself, Jack sat on the window seat and adjusted his wrinkled socks, then ran his fingers through his spiky hair.

The doorbell rang. Aunt Agatha had arrived.

***

Tap-tap went the heels of Aunt Agatha's old ankle boots as she followed Jack's mother into the sitting room. She quickly plonked herself down on the sofa, smoothed her crumpled skirt, and placed her battered leather handbag upon her bony knees. She smiled sweetly at Jack and said in her high-pitched voice, "Father O'Toole not arrived yet?"

***

"Not yet Agatha," said Jack's mother as she adjusted a couple of ornaments on the mantelpiece. "But he'll be here soon, he's never late."

"No doubt when he does arrive he'll talk a lot of hot air, he always does," said Aunt Agatha, as she cleaned her glasses and pursed her thin lips.

"He does NOT talk a lot of hot air!" said Jack's mother indignantly.

"Oh yes he does," said Aunt Agatha, replacing her glasses on to her thin nose. "You know that as well as I do, he talks nonsense, well in my opinion that means talks a lot of hot air."

Jack's mother made no further comment but instead tidied some newspapers lying on the coffee table.

Jack winked at Kojo.

Kojo sighed and stared at the flowery cushion.

The doorbell rang again.

Kojo sighed even more.

Father O'Toole had arrived.

Jack's mother rushed to open the front door.

Jack sat on his hands, swung his legs back and forth, and gazed innocently at Aunt Agatha.

Aunt Agatha peered at him over the top of her

glasses, and thought, *I've seen that innocent look on Jack's face before and it means he's up to something. Now what is he up to I wonder?*

Kojo just waited.

Jack stared at the doorway when he heard the rustle of Father O'Toole's cassock and the rattle of rosary beads.

***

With hands clasped in front of him, balding Father O'Toole glided into the room, closely followed by Jack's mother. "Good afternoon to you all," he said through his buck teeth, "I hope I find you all well and at peace with the world, yes indeed I do!"

Aunt Agatha's head jerked a response.

Jack nodded and stared at Father O'Toole's bobbing Adam's apple.

Kojo just waited some more.

"Do sit here Father," said Jack's mother, pointing to the armchair. "Your favourite seat I believe!"

"Yes indeed, indeed it is, such a comfortable

cushion. Praise be I always sit in this chair when I come for tea. You always prepare such a lovely tea for me, yes indeed, so good for the soul," said Father O'Toole.

Jack's mother blushed with pride and patted her curls.

Aunt Agatha wondered how much hot air Father O'Toole would talk today.

Jack sat quietly on the window seat and waited.

***

Slowly Father O'Toole reversed up to the chair, held on to its arms, and lowered himself down on to the flowery cushion.

Jack watched in delicious anticipation.

Kojo shut his eyes and waited.

Aunt Agatha's glasses slipped down her pointed noise as she gazed at Father O'Toole's descending bottom.

Wait for it, wait for it, any minute now! thought Jack.

Then, as Father O'Toole sat down, the whoopee cushion expelled some air with a loud gusto! Father O'Toole's face turned beetroot red and he squirmed with embarrassment which made more gustoes escape.

Jack clapped a hand over his face to stop a snort escaping.

Aunt Agatha's glasses slid clean off her nose as she sniggered.

Highly embarrassed, Jack's mother glared at Kojo.

Kojo glared back at her, he knew exactly what was coming next!

***

"OUT KOJO!" yelled Jack's mum, and pointed towards the door. "You DON'T make RUDE BODY NOISES in here!"

Kojo was already heading for the door at a steady trot, as he so often had been ordered out of the room on account of other people's rude body noises.

"So sorry about that Father, that dog has no manners. What are you feeding him on Jack? Oh I'm so embarrassed!" said Jack's mother as she wrung her hands together.

Father O'Toole sucked air in through his tombstone-like teeth, nodded and crossed his legs. The whoopee cushion let out a cracking spurt of little gustoes.

***

Jack's mother's eyebrows shot up in surprise when she heard more rude noises and was confused because Kojo had left the room! Her mouth dropped open as she slowly turned her head to stare in utter amazement at Father O'Toole.

Aunt Agatha gave Jack a knowing wink and replaced her glasses.

Jack grinned back at her.

Father O'Toole wriggled in his chair. The last gusto escaped!

Aunt Agatha looked at Father O'Toole and said, in her high-pitched voice, "What was THAT you said Father? As usual, it sounded like a lot of hot air to me."

THE END

3. Tinker, the Reindeer Who Made a Mess of Things

Young Tinker's sleigh-pulling skills were not very good, in fact they were very bad. He had practiced a lot but still made a mess of things, in fact he recently crashed on landing and got his antlers stuck in a bucket! But nevertheless he still longed to be in the team to pull Father Christmas' sleigh on Christmas Eve. *Perhaps I could get things right if I had other reindeer beside me,* thought Tinker as, leaving little hoof prints in the snow, he trotted towards the cottage.

***

Just then the cottage door opened and Father Christmas appeared. Tinker stopped mid-trot and thought, *Father Christmas is wearing his red and white suit, it must be Christmas Eve already! He's going to choose his sleigh team right now so the* other reindeer will be lined up in the paddock. And with that thought, and hope in his heart, Tinker trotted on ahead of Father Christmas. He leapt over the icy path, skidded into the snowy paddock and squeezed his little body between two tall, big-bottomed reindeer. When Father Christmas arrived young Tinker held his head up high and stood on his hoof tips to appear taller.

"Please choose me for your team," he said under his breath. Then he waited, and waited some more. But he waited in vain. Father Christmas didn't choose him, but chose the big-bottomed reindeer instead.

***

The rest of the reindeer didn't seem to mind not being chosen as they knew pulling Father Christmas' sleigh around the world was hard work, so they trotted off into the far off fields to browse the night away. But Tinker was devastated at being left out, and when the tall, big-bottomed reindeer looked down on him with smug looks on their faces as if to say, "WE have perfect sleigh skills, YOU always mess things up," he was very upset. *Nobody wants me*, thought Tinker as he stood alone, his eyes sparkling with unshed tears. Then, as the tears escaped and plopped into the snow, he watched Father Christmas harness the chosen reindeer to his toy-laden sleigh. Quickly, to hide his sadness from the others, he dashed towards the barn and kicked clods of snow out in front of him. He stamped through the barn doorway, tripped over a piglet, and somersaulted on to a pile of hay. He got up, spat hay out of his mouth, scattered the chickens and kicked over the milk churn. As he watched the milk trickle across the cobblestones he heard the musical sound of sleigh bells. Quickly he hoofed the cat aside, rushed out of the barn and gave the door a good kick on his way out. The door rebounded on to his rump, he sat down with a bump, and spun like a wooden top across the ice. He came to a stop beside wise old Buck, a recently retired reindeer.

***

Old Buck realised Tinker was upset at not being chosen to pull Father Christmas' sleigh. He was also aware young Tinker had made a mess of his landings and take-offs, but he was wise enough to know that, with practice and praise, he would get them right. Buck gave Tinker a comforting nuzzle and together they watched the reindeer pull Father Christmas' toy-laden sleigh smoothly down the icy path, up over the frozen lake and on into the starry sky. When the sleigh was out of sight and they could hear the sleigh bells no more, Tinker and Buck walked towards the barn.

Then they saw something lying in the snow beside the icy path.

The two reindeer stared down at it.

Two round eyes stared back up at them.

It was a rag doll.

***

Buck nudged Tinker, looked towards the cottage, then back again at the rag doll. Tinker knew what to do and, while Buck plodded towards the barn, he picked up the rag doll and trotted up to the cottage. He tapped on the door with his stubby antler.

Mother Christmas, known as Mama C to all reindeer, opened the door and without taking a breath, said in her rapid speech, "I made that rag doll only yesterday, she must have fallen off the sleigh, Father Christmas goes so fast on take-off as he has to deliver dolls, teddy bears, books, gadgets, electronic thingies and all sorts of toys around the world. Now let me see, who wanted this rag doll?"

She wiped her hands on her pinafore, stuffed the rag doll under her armpit, and flicked her chubby fingers through a pile of letters. "Ah, here it is... yes this is the one and it says..."

Dear Father Christmas,

Please may I have a rag doll to cuddle? I live in Snow Valley in the cabin next to the village pump under a lamp post.

Love,

Jodie

Mama C waggled the doll at Tinker. "It's up to us now to get this rag doll to Jodie tonight, so you will have to pull my sleigh we have no other option."

***

Tinker gulped and gave Mama C an anxious look. She knew he was inexperienced and perhaps would have managed to handle the sleigh with other reindeer beside him – but that was not to be, well not tonight anyway. Mama C saw anxiety in Tinker's button brown eyes and patted him on his head. "I know you've messed up a bit lately, I heard that you crashed on landing, but we have to get this doll to Jodie before daybreak and, as Buck has retired, you are the only reindeer near at hand. The others will be browsing in the fields and it will take me too long to get them back, so let's get you harnessed without further ado." She flapped her hands and shooed Tinker out of the doorway.

***

As Mama C harnessed Tinker to her small sleigh he began to quiver with nerves, because he had never taken off before with someone sitting in the sleigh, the practice sleigh had always been empty. She noticed his discomfort but said nothing as she was feeling anxious too. Nevertheless she smiled at Tinker and jumped into the sleigh.

The rag doll sat beside her.

Buck peeped round the barn door.

Mama C jiggled the reins.

"We won't arrive till we get there and if we don't hurry Father Christmas will be back before we've gone, so take off Tinker!" Mama C jiggled the reins again, which tinkled the bells.

***

Tinker stayed rooted to the spot with nerves and dug his hooves into the icy path.

"Now come along Tinker, we have to get to Snow Valley before dawn so take a deep breath and let's get going," said Mama C, and jiggled the reins yet again. Tinker, so wanting to please Mama C, took a deep breath, lowered his head and, with steam coming out of his nostrils and sleigh bells clanging, he charged down the icy path. The sleigh sprang after him, rammed his bottom and jerked him on to his knees.

The rag doll slid sideways along the seat.

Mama C went ups-a-daisy on to the sleigh floor and showed more bottom than is proper.

Tinker skidded into the red letterbox and got his nose stuck in the opening.

As Tinker yanked his nose out of the letterbox Mama C got up, sat back on the seat, then put the rag doll in her pinafore pocket. She felt sorry for Tinker but there was no other way to get the rag doll to Jodie, and at the same time, thought things weren't looking too good, in fact they were looking desperate. She looked at the crestfallen young reindeer and said kindly, "It takes practice to get it right so try again dear."

Tinker's nose throbbed and his head drooped as he dragged the sleigh back up the icy path.

***

Buck was waiting for him and gave him another comforting nuzzle.

Then Buck held his head up high and looked up at the stars.

Tinker did the same and Buck nodded his huge antlers.

Tinker knew what to do and prepared to take off again.

Buck held his breath, and watched.

Mama C held on tight, and prayed.

Tinker held his head up high, looked up at the stars and, with sleigh bells tinkling, trotted steadily down the icy path. The sleigh wobbled a bit as it rose over the frozen lake, then it rose a little bit more until Tinker was higher than he'd ever been before!

Tinker felt joy from the tip of his nose to the end of his toes.

The cool air soothed his throbbing nose.

Mama C gave a huge sigh of relief.

Below Buck nodded his huge antlers.

***

Tinker flew happily across the starry sky, and with Mama C guiding him they were soon high above the snowy plain.

Two old, shaggy polar bears, Berg and Floe, sat in the snow.

They heard the tinkling of sleigh bells and looked up.

Berg wondered where Tinker was going.

Floe thought, *Like Father Christmas, he must be going to Snow Valley as he's headed that way.*

Both bears thought he'd make a mess of the landing as they knew he had crashed into the elf laundry a while ago, and came out wearing Mama C's knickers!

The two old, shaggy polar bears chuckled and shuffled into their ice cave.

***

Soon the sleigh was above Snow Valley and Mama C peered down at the rooftops.

"I can see Jodie's snowy roof near the village pump, Father Christmas has left sleigh marks on all the others, there are none on that one so get ready to land Tinker."

From high in the starry sky Tinker looked down at Jodie's tiny, snow-covered roof and suddenly his joy vanished like a puff in the wind. Mama C noticed his anxiety and knew he didn't want to put a hoof on that tiny roof.

"If you don't land Tinker, Jodie won't have her rag

doll to cuddle and that means she will be very disappointed. Now you wouldn't want that would you?" Tinker knew Mama C was right and he had to land, somehow. He flew the sleigh lower then, as it neared Jodie's tiny roof, he stuck his legs straight out and squeezed his eyes tight shut.

***

Two fluffy white rabbits, Flake and Frost, sat in the snow and looked up. They knew Tinker was going to try and land on Jodie's roof because Father Christmas had left it out. Both rabbits thought he'd make a mess of the landing as they had heard he had only yesterday crashed into the bakery and knocked the juicy red cherries off all the sticky buns! Afraid at what might happen next, Flake and Frost covered their faces, peeped through their fluffy paws, and watched the sleigh getting lower and lower. And then, the speeding sleigh landed with a splat on Jodie's roof, bounced off, looped the loop, then fell into a snow drift beside the village pump.

***

Mama C fell out of the sleigh and tumbled, on her big bottom, down a pile of logs.

The rag doll shot out of her pocket and flew through the air.

Tinker dived antler first into the snow drift.

Flake and Frost nodded to each other and hopped off to get a closer look.

***

The silver light from the lamp post shone on Tinker's rump which was sticking out of the snowdrift. Then, as Mama C tugged on Tinker's little tail, he came out with a whoosh. She sat down with a plonk and Tinker landed on top of her. Quickly she shoved Tinker aside and looked in her pinafore pocket. It was empty. The rag doll had gone. "Oh no!" she cried. "Jodie won't have her rag doll and I have nothing else to put in her Christmas stocking."

She looked at Tinker in dismay.

Tinker looked at her in despair.

Flake and Frost looked at each other and hopped off.

***

While Tinker watched forlornly Mama C searched for the rag doll, but it was nowhere to be seen. It had disappeared. "Oh Tinker, what am I going to do?"

Tinker didn't know what Mama C could do, he felt useless and miserable. Mama C once again felt sorry for the desperate young reindeer, but she couldn't comfort him as she had problems of her own. Had she done the right thing in letting young Tinker pull her sleigh? But what else could she have done?

***

About this time, having delivered all sorts of toys and things around the world, Father Christmas arrived back in the paddock and immediately started to feed his weary reindeer with hay and carrots. Old Buck stood alone in the barn doorway and looked up at the starry sky hoping to see Tinker coming back home, but there was no sign of him. *Where could Tinker be?* he wondered, as he walked slowly towards the paddock.

Tinker had slumped down behind a hedge in Snow

Valley. A young reindeer alone with no one to comfort him. He had messed things up yet again and he supposed the tall, big-bottomed reindeer were right when they looked down on him with smug looks on their faces, as if to say they had much better sleigh skills than he had. Time dragged by as the stars began to fade and the pink dawn of Christmas Day tinged the sky. Then Tinker heard squeaks of delight.

***

He got up, peeped over the hedge, and saw Flake and Frost tossing the rag doll high up in the air between them. Tinker knew what to do and with one bound leapt over the hedge and caught the rag doll on his stubby antler. As the rag doll flopped and the rabbits hopped, he trotted proudly back to Mama C. A smile of pure joy lit up her face when she saw what Tinker had found.

"Oh Tinker, Jodie will have a rag doll after all, you really are the cleverest reindeer in the whole world!"

Tinker pricked up his ears and stared at Mama C.

Mama C sensed his pleasure and gave him a hug.

Flake and Frost watched him blink as he went quite pink.

They really didn't know what to think.

Without delay Mama C scrambled back up the pile of logs beside Jodie's cabin and put the rag doll in Jodie's stocking, which hung outside her window. Tinker, confident since Mama C had praised him and said he was the cleverest reindeer in the whole world, was eager to take off. Mama C noticed there was no sign of nerves as she harnessed him to her sleigh and said, "Father Christmas will be home by now and his reindeer will be munching their hay and carrots so let's go." Then she looked at Flake and Frost. "Come and spend Christmas with us, I've got some spare carrots in the cottage!" Always ready for a snack, the rabbits hopped into the sleigh and Mama C sat between them.

***

All three watched, a little anxiously, as Tinker, with head held high, looked up at the dawn sky. They heard the tinkle of sleigh bells, saw the toss of his stubby antlers, the quick flick of his little tail, and heard his hooves tap smartly on the icy path. Then they felt the cool air rush past their cheeks as the sleigh rose smoothly and effortlessly above Jodie's cabin, and on up into the dawn sky.

Mama C smiled. "That really was a PERFECT take-off Tinker!"

The rabbits clapped their fluffy paws together.

With joy in his heart Tinker flew over the snowy plain.

The two old shaggy polar bears, Berg and Floe, didn't see him as they were asleep in their ice cave.

Mama C relaxed in her seat.

The rabbits thought of the carrots they'd eat.

Tinker flew on towards home.

***

Mama C looked over the side of the sleigh. "Look Tinker, Father Christmas and Buck are in the paddock."

Tinker looked down.

Mama C flicked the reins and tinkled the bells.

Father Christmas looked up and was astonished to see Mama C waving at him as he thought she was up in the cottage cooking his breakfast!

But Buck smiled knowingly and nodded his huge antlers.

The tall big bottomed reindeer stopped in mid-munch and looked up at Tinker.

Tinker looked down at them and, with a smug look on his face, flew effortlessly over the frozen lake and on towards the icy path.

He's going to land, thought Flake and Frost, and together they began to shake.

"Don't you two go worrying yourselves now?" said Mama C. "Tinker is going to make a PERFECT landing."

And do you know, that's exactly what Tinker did.

THE END

Printed in Great Britain
by Amazon